in Prose

Kasia Buczkowska

Un-Gyve *Press*

Library of Congress Control Number:
2013947646

ISBN: 978-0-9829198-3-5

10 9 8 7 6 5 4 3 2 1

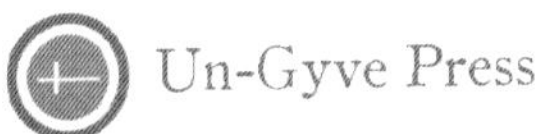

Designed by Un-Gyve Limited.

The title typeface is Bodoni, Giabattista Bodoni, and Garamond, designed after the original Claude Garamond types, is used for the text throughout.

Christopher Ricks is the Literary Advisor to Un-Gyve Press, an independent imprint of The Un-Gyve Limited Group.

Un-Gyve Press Boston
www.un-gyvepress.com

The Un-Gyve Limited Group
139A Charles Street, No. 393
Boston, Massachusetts 02114-3282 U.S.A.

To my mother Irena.

Contents

IV

V

VI

in Prose

I

Success

"My horse lost the race and he is out of sorts," a stable-boy says, grooming the tousled mane. "I keep consoling him, so he does not get discouraged." He kisses the horse on his muzzle. "Today you are a loser, understand?" he says, "but only for today."

Nearby a horse kicks about and neighs in desperation. He jumped obstacles and fences flawlessly, yet he angrily gnaws at the wooden logs of the enclosure.

"That horse won the race and he is out of sorts," says the stable-boy of the loser horse. "His owners went for cocktails to celebrate their victory." The horse hustles about and rears. Swollen veins mark his neck.

"The creature got some applause and now he stands in solitude."

The cats that calm the horses have waned into startled eyes in dark corners of the stable.

Memories

This parrot, like all parrots, has a perfect memory. She greets you with "Good morning" and says "Good bye" for farewell. When music plays, she whistles and swings to all sides. At times she barks. At times she imitates the swishing sound of a sword. At times, she utters a curse. Nobody has been sick for a long time and she still coughs. When she sees a warm embrace, she sighs.

For quite some time she has been plucking her feathers. Perhaps she is worried about the state of the world or the on-going war in the Garden of Eden. She used to cover a big distance with one smooth flight, now she drops to the floor half-way with a fearful thump. She walks on the floor, as if surprised that the flight was unsuccessful. At times, she pretends that the flight was meant to be that short and says "Good bird" for encouragement. She repeats such half-failed flights a few times a day.

She remembers the taste of a banana or a grapefruit: when she sees the fruit, she makes her presence known. She remembers what jealousy is: when you hold a conversation, she creates havoc. She fails to remember only one thing: to fly, a bird has to have healthy wings.

An Order

"She likes caresses," a farmer says, scratching her pig behind its ear. The pig is making grunting noises. "She loves being tickled on the sides the most." The woman strokes the animal on its massive back, moving her hand from side to side. With her fingers she doodles on the pig's pale pink skin. Delicately, stronger, delicately. The beast twists its body and wriggles. Whenever the woman takes her hand away, the pig knocks against the wooden fence and thrusts up its chin in expectation, asking for more.

"There are orders already placed on her," the farmer says. "These parts," she circles around both sides of the spine, "a restaurant will take, and the ribs the fire department will take for a picnic. My pigs live six months. They are very affectionate and docile. The unfortunate part is that we kill them."

The pig stands still, looking up at the starry sky.

"She's had a wonderful life."

Tenant

At night she woke me up with rustling noises. She shredded newspapers and some of my notes. She took bites out of my bananas. To show the mouse politely to the door, I removed all temptations. She would be starving and leave the premises herself. The creature however proved to be creative. I caught her hanging on a curtain and nibbling at the leaves of my favorite plant. Lack of respect for the world of flora made me furious.

A good strategy and a skill of a detective were needed. I researched the market for mouse traps. Unfortunately all carried cruelty.

Why doesn't she move to the park or the neighbors, I thought.

During my absence she ate half of my bitter chocolate and from my woolen sock made herself a lodging. Revenge and mercy tormented me in turns. And joy that a wild animal feels happy at my home. And fascination with what the mouse would do next.

Sometimes she would disappear, to my appeasement. Or perhaps she watched a film with me, hiding in some corner? When out of a sudden something scampered off, I panicked that it could be a member of her family moving in. Where does tolerance end and war begin?

An animal would do anything to survive. Once sitting in an armchair, I pretended that I was dozing off. The mouse climbed onto my desk and keeping her front paws on a book and stretching her neck, she kept observing me. Was she about to outwit me in some way? We were cheating one another. My heart softened, but the rodent remained a nuisance.

Treat

The turkey follows Billy everywhere. Billy saved its life, when other farmers had written the ill and weak bird off. At night Billy gave it some liquor to soothe the pain. During daytime, he fed it a concoction from his organic garden. Screeching and whimpering noises turned into joyful gobble.

Billy communicated with animals perfectly. He avoided people, because he could not read them. That's the way he was born.

The turkey became a picture of health. As a special treat Billy promised the turkey a Thanksgiving trip. He decided to show to his kindred spirit a little bit of the South.

On the road, through the wide open windows of the car, they enjoyed the warm breeze; it caressed their foreheads. Country music played. Excited by the views, the turkey ruffled up its feathers and pinched Billy's elbow tenderly. From time to time the car did not exactly follow a straight line.

Suddenly a police car appeared out of nowhere. A policeman stopped their car, looked at them with a cold stare and gave them a ticket.

"Why?" Billy asked repeatedly. Reasoning was not his strength. Confused, Billy and the turkey wrinkled their foreheads, looked at each other baffled. Perhaps the policeman had seen a turkey only on a plate.

The Fly Bit the Cow

A cow stood on the grass. Grandma was milking the cow. The milk was flowing into the bucket. A fly was cruising around the cow. Granddaughter was chasing the fly with a birch branch. "Grandma, where is God?" "God lives in your heart and he will always whisper to you whenever you move away from him." The cow was stretching its ear. "God is also in this grass, on which the bucket stands, and in this milk that fills the bucket to the brim, and in this cow that gives the milk, and everything wants to live its own life." The cow nodded. The girl held the branch still. The fly bit the cow. The irritated cow swung its tail. Grandma knocked over the bucket. The milk spilled on the grass. "Nobody will drink milk today. Everything has its boundaries," Grandma said. The cow nodded.

He hid his face in his big hands. He cried because he had sold his six horses.

"How are those different hands now treating my horses?"

He worked with the horses together, in the field they planted topinambur, in the forest they cut down larch wood.

"When we parted, I told them why we could no longer be together," he explained. "I kissed them one by one. Our tears were falling loudly onto the carpet of conifer needles."

On a piece of napkin, he was drawing in detail to explain how a larch tree gets an artery blockage, when a deer eats its leafy rosette.

"Sometimes a tree is dying of a heart attack, like a man, and you need to rescue it."

His half-a-century face became more and more inflamed as he said that just as it is important to feed horses high quality oats, and absolutely necessary to boil the oats, and indispensable to give them mineral salt lick, it is equally important to give them a big dose of human love.

"A horse is a sly animal. You caress one, and the other one is rolling its eyes, but do not be fooled that they all would fall for a sugar cube. They differ like people."

He apologized profusely for burdening me with his emotions and said: "I am modest, resistant to cold and vermin, like topinambur; I can live on every soil; I am knowledgeable; I like ironing my shirts; I love women and I admire breasts of every size, I'm looking for a woman who can carry my crying over horses."

Advice

He held crayons in his tiny hands.

"Grandma, I've got this big problem."

He stood by the table anxiously.

"In kindergarten, there is this girl I like. I don't tell her, I just look at her."

He spilled the crayons onto the table and supported his head on his palms, as if it weighed too much.

"I would like to draw something for her or sing a song for her. I would like to give her flowers, like Grandpa gives to you. I would like to kiss her. I'll show you how."

He came up to her, brushed her hair off her cheek.

"Like this," he kissed her.

He was looking at her face for a moment and then took her cheeks between his palms.

"Or straight on the lips, like Grandpa kisses you. Like this," he kissed her.

She covered her astonishment with a smile.

"If I may give you any advice," she tried sounding resolute "it is not to overdo it. There is no need to hurry. Just start with the crayons, choose the colors you like and draw her something special. Let her enjoy it and see how she responds."

He was staring at her face and suddenly started gathering crayons from the table. He looked slightly perturbed.

"I wonder why you don't advise Grandpa not to overdo it. You, Grandma, can't see anymore how Grandpa chases after you."

Snowdrops

In Morningside Park, winter and spring are in eerie harmony. Snowdrops peek through snow shimmering in feverish sun. Teenagers walk vigorously and speak with fervor. Two giggling girls arm-in-arm lag behind.

"Your spaghetti strap has slipped," a boy says to one of the girls, dribbling a basket-ball around her feet.

"It's supposed to be like that," the girl says.

"I like bare arms and long skirts, but aren't you a bit cold?"

"I'm not interested in boys," the girl says.

The boy bounces the ball closer to the girl's feet. "I'd pick a snowdrop for you, but they are an endangered species."

"I'm not interested in boys."

"How do you know?"

"I just know," the girl giggles, looking at her friend and pulling her closer.

The boy dribbles the ball in various positions. He lets the ball out in front of him, catches up with it and throws it into an imaginary basket under the azure sky. "I'm interested in girls."

"Good for you."

"I know you don't know you don't know."

"How do you know I don't know
I don't know?"

"I just know." The boy dribbles back and forth, spinning.

The girl puts on dark sun glasses and looks ahead, "Yes and no and I don't know."

"They bother me because I'm a foreigner. They blame me for starting the war."

"Which war?" his mother asked.

"They don't exactly say which one."

"So why did you invite them to your birthday party?" irritated, she proceeded to straighten his paper crown with the many-colored jewels painted on it.

"Because I like them, even if they bother me."

The mother disappeared in the corridor. She tidied the visitors' shoes into neat rows, which were left in disarray. "Shoes off," she told the kids coming in, who took them off reluctantly. "I won't clean after you."

The boy came into the corridor. He grabbed a shoe cleaning stool, took his mother by the hand and brought her to the middle of the living room.

"My dear guests," he spoke loudly, climbing onto the stool, to be for once taller than the rest, "before we eat my birthday cake, I'm going to sing you a song about a river, in my language, which my mother taught me."

When he finished singing, there was silence. Abashed, he jumped off the stool and hid under the table.

"Hey, so what happened to that river? And how do you say *river* in your language? And how do you say…?" the kids shouted questions over each other. They stormed after him under the table and they did not come out from there for a long time.

Size of a Feeling

This child is brilliant but difficult. She learns easily, but does not listen. She frolics when the hour is not for it. Contrary, disobedient, merciless. You wilt.

At night, when she is falling asleep, she says: "I love you so much like from here to the sky."

Cemetery

On the walkway at Wall Street, tourists rest on benches in the shape of gold ingots. A bank neighbors a bank. Pedestrians buy souvenirs, snacks and ice creams of various flavors. Tired by the swelter, a policeman is leaning on his M16.

Behind a wall, in the courtyard of a church, kindergarten children play. They run in the alleys, calling out: "Who's the monster now?", and scare one another. There are many volunteers for the role.

On a path near a headstone with an engraved epitaph "Gone to the Grave with Pride", a girl is drawing a sun with chalk. In front of the grave of a veteran of the War of Independence, two kids scuffle.

At noon the church bell rings out and for a while softens construction sounds coming from the plaza where two towers stood.

"In five minutes we'll gather kids and leave the cemetery," kindergarten teachers arrange.

"Teacher, what is a cemetery?" asks the girl who was painting a sun.

Subway Jazz

On the subway platform, a little girl was entertaining her younger brother in a stroller. She was trotting in a dance-like manner, made figures and turns. The boy watched amused and licked a red lollipop. Their mother dressed in tight jeans and with huge headphones over her ears, leaned against the stroller, swinging her body.

The train arrived. The woman grabbed her daughter's hand and just as she pushed the stroller inside the car, the lollipop fell out of the toddler's hand onto the tracks. Instantly the boy started screaming. The mother did not respond. She sat her daughter next to her. The boy cried more and more. Dozing off passengers were opening their tired eyes. The mother, with listening, slightly absent eyes, raised her warning finger to the child to calm down, to no avail.

"Digital generation," remarked a lady to another lady, with disapproval.

"Today people do not fight for anything. Especially manners," reacted an elderly lady in a Sherlock Holmes hat. "Kids are treated like adults, and from adults you expect less than from children."

Crying was turning into whining. A man in a well-tailored suit was tapping his rolled up newspaper against his lap. The heads of passengers were rising from above papers, books, to exchange bitter expressions. One woman remained unmoved in her knitting.

A man with wild hair, in pajama bottoms featuring bears and reindeer, tried to distract the toddler, also to no avail.

The little girl looked up at her mother several times, and seemed to be embarrassed for her toddler brother.

"Be quiet right now! Forget the lollipop! Can't you see mummy is listening to jazz!" she yelled.

In an old home movie, she shows what kind of butterfly bow she made for her doll. She explains why she scolded her toy dog. She says what difficulty she ran into and how she solved it. She shares her feelings with enthusiasm.

Today she wrote in her calendar: "I have no will to live."

Something broke in her, some thread has torn, said those who knew her well.

"What's up?"

"Nothing."

"What are you doing?"

"Nothing." She'd give faded responses.

From specialists she heard: disease, depression.

Medications have dulled her senses, she has lost the ability to cry and reflect.

One day while roaming with no aim, she ran into a woman and hardly noticed when they began to chat.

The woman looked at her warmly. "Sometimes a person falls into a pit," she said, "because in a hunt for something, she loses her own path, or becomes deaf or blind to the surrounding world, or talks herself into some nonsense, or forgets what is true and important. Such a state is a signal from within that something in your inner self wants to wake up, break free."

She felt that the woman was talking to her for real, reaching the depths of her interior.

"Feelings are not a puddle of flat water, they are a mountain range: here smooth, ragged there; they are summits, flatlands, valleys. And pain is a part of life not to be feared, because fear destroys you. Perhaps part of you is craving to bloom…." With hypnotically apt words the woman was transporting her into some other place.

Home she went.

"What's up?"

"I'm alive."

"What are you doing?"

"Lazing about … reading and drinking bitter herbs and then I'm running to teach kids to sing."

Shame

"You are looking at a hungry man," he spoke to commuters. He was squeezing through the crowded subway car, with a tin can of jingling coins.

"I'm ashamed to beg. My name is … never mind," he stopped and pointed to a passenger.

"It's a disgrace! A fellow man with a baby in hand, standing, and you just sit there, unable to relinquish one seat. Look at yourselves, people! You call yourselves Christians, Muslims, Jews, and other predilections, you'll go to your places of worship, and I'm ashamed right now to say I'm a New Yorker."

Some seated passengers looking straight ahead dropped their eyes to look at the floor; some looking at the floor looked up straight ahead; a few looked up at the man's haggard face.

"I don't even feel like begging. Have a good weekend. God bless you." He left the car at the nearest station.

Prosperity

After many years they looked at each other across the table.

"You haven't changed at all."

"You haven't changed as well."

He had a scarf knotted according to the latest fashion. He sat proud about his appearance, his perfume, his car, his driver, his gardener, his stocks. He said that he traverses the continents, talks to very important people, stays at the best hotels.

He gave his watch a prolonged look.

"I bet you still don't have a TV," he asked.

"I do, but I rarely use it," she said, surprised.

"You know that I've always had a mercantile attitude towards life."

"Oh really?"

"Whatever I am to promote, diamonds, vacuum cleaners, plastic, I always follow the demand and supply curve," he said.

"I've always admired your … ambition," she said with a smile.

He seemed to have it all, yet something was extinguished, she thought. Perhaps he has become a yes man.

Mansions

"You could have been a diplomat, a businessman with a mansion, a doctor with a private plane, a banker, and you became a poet," a father used to say to his son.

The father lived in a palace, had a fortune, but his heart was rather stingy and sad. He wished his son had his own palace, but the son loved life of a different kind.

"What an oaf." The father did not consider writing poetry a worthy occupation.

A comfortable armchair, a costly suit, services and well-traveled roads would not suffice for the son. He fancied uncertainty, fortuity and risk. Surprises, not statistics.

"Father, I'm going to travel the world."

"Off you go!" The father slammed a heavy door behind him.

In the countryside the son gathered gooseberries to earn a living. He wrote about rural life, about beauty and how he betrayed his love. When in a country of prosperity he became homeless, he wrote about things intangible that many feel, about his own and others' wounds that do not bleed. About a night spent on the street, on a frozen bird for a pillow. About a happy coincidence.

When the son read his poems on TV, the father deemed writing poetry a worthy occupation. Now that he is no longer able to stroll his palace's numerous chambers, he lies in bed and reads his son's verses. What can a man smuggle to the other side of life but a few words.

He got disappointed by many verdicts. Justice often escaped the rule of law. Today he earns his living delivering food at night.

"I feed New York," he says with pride. "I see the city in its intimacy and there's no end to my delight."

"An elegant lady in a flowing dress opens the door for me. Under her feet a beautiful Arabic mosaic. Where is she going? Where has she come from? With a graceful gesture she takes my delivery. We exchange four words and smiles.

An apartment in disarray. A toddler runs up to me and shows me a blue pear he drew. He relishes my praise. In the back, a decorated Christmas tree … in the middle of the summer. Is Christmas time every day in this home?

In the door of a shady building, a girl stands, all dolled up, dressed in a skimpy sequined top, and a boy in a baseball cap, bare feet, with a guitar slung across his naked chest. She fixes her hairdo; he pulls up his low-hanging pants. They look for cash awkwardly, their speech is slurred: 'Music does not glue today, brother.'

I deliver a few meals to a corner and receive payment in counterfeit bills.

A modest room in silence, a lamp lit up, the floor covered with books. A writer invites me for a brief chat over a cup of jasmine tea. He says that the night air contains fewer disturbances and it's easier to connect with the cosmos. He hands me his latest poem: 'Next time, with the sandwich, please bring me your impressions. I'll be grateful.' "

"What do you see in this delivery of sandwiches?" his friends ask with a note of irony.

"I've always been interested in otherness."

"My father died on me, just like that," he pounded his fists together. "He went for a stroll in the garden and left without a word. One day there, then … do you understand?"

His glassy eyes highlighted his broken nose. Distended veins on his forearm wound like many rivers. Recently his drinking sprees ended in blackouts. "Have you come to your senses yet?" his family and friends kept asking him.

"How can I come to my senses, with this suffocating pain in my chest? Nobody in the ring has ever given me such a blow." He sprang up from the sofa, walked about the room with a light step of a boxer, and sat down.

"If I could tell you how much I loved my father, I would, but I cannot." He hit his open palm with his fist. "He was the only one who understood me, even though I was not an easy man. My father was quiet but firm. He knew how to measure things. He had to. In the mine he worked with explosive materials. Maybe that's why he understood me, because I am one, too," he laughed to himself. "But he knew that I never raised my hand at anybody, unless someone meddled with me."

He got up, made a circle, and sat down. "Once I pushed my teacher into the swimming pool because he pulled me by my ear to show off in front of some school girls in skimpy swimsuits. I cannot stand violence without good reason," he

punched the air. "One day there, then....
Understand?"

"He has not died, he has become part of you," I said, as I could say nothing else. He was stroking his fist.

"Did you tell your father how much you loved him?"

"I did not need to tell him that. I had proved it to him. If that man had left without the certainty that I loved him, till the end of my life I'd be my own punching bag."

He brought a drink of raspberry color, "This will warm us up."

They talked about this and that.

"Apart from the fact that I have no front tooth, I have this vice that … – just do not be scared – I have been in the can."

With a slightly sweeping movement he sat down on the sofa next to her. He looked at the buttons of her sweater, then closely examined the seams.

Alcohol, no tooth, late hour, touches the buttons…, worried she was summing up in her mind.

"Exactly such sweaters I used to knit in the can. The seams are done decently, but these two buttons, I can see, you have sewn by yourself."

"Mhhmmm," she agreed.

"You see, not very professionally. Buttons should have freedom, not too close to the sweater and not too far."

He walked her to the subway and waited until the train came.

"If you want these buttons done properly, please ask me to do it for you. I want to feel needed and know that I came out as a worthwhile man."

A Piece of Your Orange

Hurriedly I moved away from a huge crane that was lifting iron beams in its teeth. I like to avoid construction scaffoldings, hammer drills, columns of steam belching from under the streets, buckets of concrete hanging in the air.

I was peeling an orange as I walked.

"Could you share a piece of your orange?" asked a man with bravura. His pants were densely mottled with paint. His foot in a heavy boot, with untied shoelace, rested on a hydrant. In this club pose, he smoked a cigarette nonchalantly.

"Sure," I said.

"Oh, no, thank you," he demurred with an easy smile.

"Here you are," I said, stretching out my hand with the offering.

"Thank you, really. I just wanted to check the state of your heart."

IV

Last Day of Summer

A lake, trees, tranquility.

Someone is strolling along the lake and with a measuring eye is looking at the horizon. Someone is holding her cheek to the sun and a book on her lap. Someone is fishing, barely visible in high wetland. Someone wonders aloud about real estate in that area. Someone is listening to silence.

"I'll swim across the lake on this last day of summer," he took off his clothes, stood up facing the lake, straight, and moved his limbs a bit to warm up.

"The dancer still has the body of a teenager," someone commented. "Firm all over."

By the lake he took off his shoes and jumped into the water.

"High time to buy new shoes!" someone shouted, to everyone's amusement.

"What do you see that we don't see?" someone asked the painter.

"Well, I don't really know.... You look at these shoes, that they are all crumpled, creased and old, and I'm looking at the light crawling over them."

A Few Trees

While he was finishing work on his new summer house, he dreamed up the idea of a pond. To make more space at the edge of his property, he moved the wall of the forest slightly.

"I cut out a few trees," he said matter-of-factly.

From that moment, he had experienced no peace. He constantly had uninvited guests.

One day a bear welcomed itself into the man's attic. The beast searched through whatever was under the roof and left the place in a considerable mess.

Just when the attic was restored to order, a skunk invited himself to the basement. The man tried to scare it off with loud heavy rock. Incidentally, he matched the creature's taste.

Then a gang of bumblebees flew into the house. They fancied curtains of imported fabric with plant motifs. They sat on the flowers and tried to pollinate them.

As soon as the pond had taken shape, frogs covered it all in spawn.

In the evenings, whenever the man went out to sit on the porch, an owl seemed to cast at him a judgmental look.

"It's hard to fight nature," he sighed.

A Solid Home

She says that she had an ideal husband: "Caring, homebound, educated, only could not take contradiction." He used to hang necklaces around her neck. He brought apricots to bed. When she was cold, he would bundle her up in a camel blanket. He told her she was shapely even when she got round. "Caring, homebound, educated, only could not take contradiction." He used to make all kinds of repairs, polished things. For their daughter, he knitted a skirt full of flowers. For their son, he built a boat with a strong sail. "Caring, homebound, educated, only could not take contradiction." He was precise in speech: he pierced the essence of things with words. He was so precise in movement that with scissors he cut mosquitoes in half in their flight. With pride he told his friends how he assisted his wife at their children's birth. He sculpted his muscles with utmost care: "Soul and body, body and soul" – he agreed with the ancient thinkers. "Caring, homebound, educated ..." One day, she opened the door and left forever. He blew up the house to pieces.

"So tell me…, are you my daughter or my granddaughter?"

"Granddaughter, Grandma."

"Granddaughter. My beloved granddaughter." She was looking into my face with warmth in her eyes. "Very good." Reassured in the facts, she returned to peeling vegetables. "Just after we finish making the soup, I'm going to give you something. A necklace of raw amber."

"You've already given it to me. It's exquisite. I tell everybody it's a present from you."

"Well, no need to tell it to everybody." She laughed with restraint, but joy was present in her voice.

Moderation and restraint ruled her life. When I was a child, I was fascinated with how she could make something out of nothing. In her house nothing was ever wasted. I loved listening to her stories about which vegetables get along well and which ones do not like growing in each other's company and why. "Some of it is science and some of it is my own philosophy," she would emphasize. The vegetables competed with each other in quality and quantity, just to get into Grandma's good graces. Cucumbers multiplied. Leaves of lettuce stood fluffed up, robust and fresh. The dill showed off the most, to the point of going wild beyond the border of the garden. While weeding, Grandma digressed. "A good garden is like a good life," she used to say. "It depends on subtleties."

"I'll turn down the radio," my mother said.

"Please do not, they're singing beautifully," said Grandma and joined in the singing.

"And I'll be the second chorus," volunteered my father.

Grandma's notes rose higher than ever. It seemed that the instrument ignored the limit of its abilities. When she finished singing, she swiftly rose up from the chair and pointed to the boiling broth. We put vegetables into the pot with pieces of chicken.

"Chicken feet add this special flavor to the broth," she explained. "But if you could see," she laughed out loud, "what sort of rumpus your mother made about chicken feet. She ran away from kindergarten, when she had not gotten chicken feet. If she had demanded the breast or the chicken leg, but no, she fancied chicken feet! In rebellion, she ran away. She always knew what she wanted. This was the first injustice she experienced, or perhaps malice."

Grandma raised a spoon to her mouth to taste the broth.

"Oh, Grandma, it still needs to be cooked." I grabbed the spoon away from her lips.

"I used to know everything, and now absolutely nothing," she said in a tone of resignation.

"Grandma, am I your daughter or your granddaughter?" I asked her.

She looked at me with a smile of sympathy. "If I'm Grandma, then you are Granddaughter. It could not be more logical."

"You see, Grandma, you remember. You remember a lot of things."

"You are clowning around," she was amused. "And the second injustice," she went on, "which your mother suffered was that year after year, during Christmas time, she was sitting with her nose pressed against the window and wept when a priest going from door to door to bless every home, passed by our house, because there were two religions under our roof. I a Catholic and Grandpa a Russian Orthodox. I still do not know if then I explained it all well to her," she got lost in her thoughts for a moment.

"I cannot imagine, Grandma, not having two Christmases and two Easters every year."

"You see. Neither can I. It is unthinkable. And how we were crazily in love with each other. We married in secrecy, against our families' convictions, and for a few days we had to stay in hiding."

My mother was standing at the window and was looking into the distance. We all heard this episode for the first time. With time Grandma showed less and less restraint in revealing details of her life.

"But why am I standing idly?" she pointed to her feet on the floor. "Why nobody gives me anything to do?" she said it so convincingly that everybody started looking around the kitchen for an activity. My father gave her a bowl of apples to peel and asked with a chuckle: "Ma, are these apples or oranges?"

"Apples, by definition," she waved at him with dismissive humor.

The apples were imperfect, with blemishes, from an unsprayed garden, but their aroma filled the entire kitchen.

"So tell me…, are you my daughter or my granddaughter?"

Irreconcilable Differences

She admired moss growing wild. He admired neat flowerbeds. She walked away from him.

He opened envelopes carelessly. She opened envelopes carefully with an ivory knife. She walked away from him.

She was crazy about one writer's penmanship. He could not see what she could see. He walked away from her.

He was moved easily. She wept only at funerals. He walked away from her.

He liked laugh-lines around women's eyes. She kept on smoothing herself. She walked away from him.

She cut carrots lengthwise. He cut carrots breadthwise. He walked away from her.

He and she agreed on everything, each walking away from each other.

To the Last Moment

I was fired from work. I gave away my whole self, but my bosses were cold and stiff. They told me that I was slightly off and frivolous. Slightly off? People, a little bit of metaphysics, please! Who was dead around there?

They thought that a man … click and is dead, because our poor instruments indicate no activity. But I felt that in these people their soul still lives, that still there is life in their cells. In work I followed common sense and my intuition. What, was I supposed to pretend – that they are not there? These were my clients.

I could see that a grandpa was slightly uncomfortable, because the collar bothered his neck. When a man crosses to the other world, then you can choke him? I loosened his collar a bit. I turned around and I heard a quiet "God, bless you" behind my back. The colds and stiffs immediately denied it. But if one does not want to hear something, then one will not hear it. These people talk when nobody asks them to. All my grandparents are already in the other world, but I hear their voices. They help me make big decisions.

One day I heard feeble sighs. I approached the woman and could feel that she craved a caring touch. I put my hand on her blue dress, right next to her heart and I held for a short while and could see that radiance entered her face. And suddenly the cold one grabs me by my collar. He nearly accused me of molesting her. Does anybody in this world still know the difference between caring and molesting?

I noticed sad lips. I sang to this boy a few good hits, about staircase to heaven, about days we still do not know, and his face immediately brightened. The corners of his lips raised. But if one does not want to see something, then one will not see it. The stiffo said that I was not serious. What, am I supposed to be as serious as a funeral parlour?

For this child that has not had a chance to experience frolics, I acted out a few fables. The little one did not make a sound, but I could feel signals flowing from her heart to my heart. Indifference is the worst thing. Most of people in their lives walk in coma.

After indifference, boredom is the worst. Sometimes I would tell jokes to this guy who looked bored. He grimaced. I tried harder, more refined ones until I saw approval. I also practiced public speaking about current affairs. Now with my solid arguments I can beat every president.

I knew I was doing something good, because I felt my blood stirring. Literally I felt I was levitating.

Of course, I did not resurrect them completely, but I know that to their last moment I gave my whole self to them, according to common sense and my intuition. And who can show me exactly where one ends and the other begins! I have not lived two decades yet, but I have seen people go away and only now I am ready for life.

Christmas Spirit

An elderly woman was slowly walking up the stone stairs of the library. With a cane in her hand, she was holding on to the railing. In the other hand she held an umbrella and a large bunch of white flowers.

"I rescued some flowers!" she said beaming with joy. Breathing heavily she looked at the few steps left to climb.

"Across the street," she pointed with her cane, "there was a Christmas party. People grabbed their gift baskets, full of perfumes, trinkets and gadgets and discarded the flowers in the trash."

She reached the landing and put her dripping umbrella next to her modest lodging by the wall. "I could not rescue them all. They showed great disrespect for the flowers!" she shook her head. "Would you like one?"

"Thank you. I'll take the one with a broken stem," I said. "What are you going to do with them?"

"I will be enjoying them."

The evening wore the darkest shade of black. The snow was changing into rain midflight. The lions frozen in stone were guarding the library and the woman with white flowers. I thought about bringing her warm socks and hot cocoa.

For days and days the broken flower she gave me refused to wilt.

V

"There is something missing in these potato pancakes. Potatoes, flour, onion, salt …" aloud he enumerated the ingredients. "I must have forgotten something."

"Nothing is missing," I reassured the host.

He liked indulging himself with cuisine, but most of all entertaining his friends to his home-made dishes.

"Being retired, when you can no longer dash ahead you tend to look into the past. Our post-war generation still remembers hunger. Did my mother add whole eggs or just yolks?" he looked at his potato pancake which did not seem to diminish.

Potato pancakes melted away in my mouth to full satisfaction, and words wished to remain silent.

"Even though all the products in them are the best quality …" he waved his fork, disconsolate, kept putting it away on the table and picking it up again.

"Actually, mother, you did not spoil us with food," he spoke to a framed photograph of his mother and father sitting at a table and smiling away from beyond. "If you think about it, at home we had either potatoes or potato pancakes, alternating with dumplings or noodles, and not much else. Everything cooked with second-rate oils, as olive oil was a pipe-dream. Nothing special, yet everything tasted delicious," he seemed to search for the love with which his mother served him food.

Diagnosis

A problem disturbed a certain man. He was losing more and more hair. He turned to experts to find the cause.

A doctor profusely advertised prescribed a bag of pills and a high bill for a one-minute visit.

A psychotherapist popular on TV stated that it was due to a childhood episode which required a long-term treatment.

A man behind the counter of a trendy shop, who had previously sold guns in Texas, praised tonics and gels, whose ingredients he could not pronounce, but he guaranteed results.

A priest immediately sensed skepticism toward faith and devised a pilgrimage up a mountain on foot.

A personal stylist recommended transferring hair from a more hidden place.

A professor, a star of academia, analyzed the problem in a postmodern manner into a dozen theories, all relative.

A poet spoke metaphorically that he needlessly turned his head-dress into a feather duster.

A totally bald guru said calmly to let the hair simply fall out.

From the multitude of opinions the man's hair stands on end. Only his comb remains silent and shows its last four teeth.

Beyond Pain

When my mother beat me as a little boy, I did not feel great anger. But when she beat my hunch-backed grandmother, I trembled from rage. My mother went crazy from love when an officer abandoned her. I remember playing with his shiny gun. My father, who had died in the war, is a fleeting memory. I cannot recall his face, just the feeling of us three lying happy in bed.

Forever, I tried to understand why she was short on love for me. And the mother of my mother loved me beyond life.

Once, in church, I admitted to my mother that I had stolen a box of matches. I explained I loved the shapely little box and the order inside it. She started to strike me and whacked me solidly a few times. Never mind that under a roof of a temple. Apparently she was religious.

Already then when I was five, people called me "uncle." I had to fend for myself.

When I left a Soviet jail, my grandma greeted me. Tears dripped from her blind eyes. She told me that she prayed for me in two ways: so I do not die, or so that dear God would take me to save me from torture. It is bizarre that I survived. I spared her the stories about violence and humiliation. The pain that was strangely more gentle than that when your mother does not love you.

Blind Love

For his birthday, the grandchildren gave their grandfather a watch. "Thank you," he said, "it's beautiful. Indeed, however … my old watch runs precisely, it's faultless."

The new watch ended up in the drawer.

The next year the grandchildren bought the grandfather a color TV set. He smiled and thanked them with his eyes slightly lowered. "Hmmm," he said then, "it's a bit too colorful. This black and white one shows the world clearly and you can see what's important."

The new TV landed on the floor in the corner.

For his following birthday they bought him a state-of-the-art bicycle. "An impressive construction, certainly," the grandfather said, admiring it. "You must have spent a fortune. My old bike will be offended."

"My grandchildren love me, without completely understanding," grandfather said to himself, sipping tea from his favorite tin mug.

Independence

During the war they killed her mother, father, sister and brother. She was left alone as a ten-year old girl with big hazel eyes and uncertain steps. She hid in attics, cellars and pits in the ground. She saw plenty in concentration camps. For many years strangers helped her make her braids.

I look at her in astonishment. She is always merry, walks with a dance-like step, consoles others, sends smiles around, as if nothing unfortunate has ever happened to her.

In talks about pain, you hear confessions: who suffered what, from whom, in what places and circumstances; here and there someone waves fists in the air. They weigh and compare their suffering.

"Why aren't you complaining, why aren't you accusing anybody, but instead pretending and ignoring your pain when among them all you suffered the most?"

"Long time ago I promised myself to be independent from hatred, because in difficult moments the easiest thing is to succumb to hatred. And all my life I tried to hold on to that promise," she responds with a smile.

"But you lost everybody and wherever you are, you give love away?"

"When I see hatred, I kill it with love, because there is no other way."

For Dasha Werdygier-Rittenberg

"So … how about one?"

"Today you were supposed to quit," she said firmly.

"You're right. You're right."

She was feeding him, as he could no longer direct his hand to his mouth successfully. He ate like a baby, who is just learning to eat from a spoon. His head swang loosely. His body refused to take anything in.

"You are a sweetie pie. Thank you for feeding me."

"From now on you will not drink!" she said even more firmly. She felt disgust towards her bans and orders.

"I have to listen to you because I love you," he was staring into the floor.

He said it with such honesty that she started believing that at last he'd surrender. She had no more patience, but kept trying.

"You are such a substantial man. You have so many talents, and you drown everything in alcohol."

"You're right. You're right … You know how much I love you. From the first sight. I will do anything for you."

"You must stop drinking first of all for yourself."

"Oh, yes, for myself too," he was looking at her helplessly. They sat in silence for a moment.

"And when I don't drink, am I handsome?"

"Of course you are."

"So … how about one?"

"Why do you drink?" she ignored his question with a question.

"I have some problem."

"What problem?"

"I have no breaks. When I start, I just keep on. With me, it does not end with one."

"You need to use breaks."

"You're right. You're right … I'm going to unrubble my room from bottles. So … how about one?"

Rescued

She woke up dead. Dead, because how could she have been alive, if she were indifferent to everything. Nothing fascinated her, nothing made her laugh, nothing irritated her, nothing moved her.

With an effort she lifted a trash bag and left the house. In the garbage can there were worn out shoes, potato peels, a shattered mirror, an old calendar with notes, computer interior organs, pomegranate shells and a book *Immortal Poems*. With an effort she lifted the book and came back home.

Till the end of that day she read the poems. She fell asleep alive.

VI

Riches

"How poorly they live, our grandma and grandpa," someone visiting my grandparents said in an undertone. It was a sentence I heard in my childhood and it stang me to the core. I remember glancing askance at the owner of those words.

Poorly? Entire days I would sit on the porch leading to the house, under the spell of the wealth.

Along the soil-covered cellar, sunflowers grew. Their radiant sunny heads served as a paradise for bees which migrated acrobatically from flower to flower. At the end of the row of sunflowers, rhubarb grew, which had apparently sowed itself there. I stared at its thick crimson stalks and large dark-green leaves and pondered the so self-sown a display. The cellar hid infinity: jars of marinated mushrooms and pickled cucumbers; potatoes; cabbages; cauliflowers; apples in many hues; preserves of forest berries. My grandparents showered their guests with gifts of the soil.

Behind the wooden fence, on the neighbors' pasture, handsome horses grazed. They would approach each other and cuddle up; at times one would gustily gallop away, but not for long.

The path through the garden of blooms and butterflies led to a brook. Its banks were strewn with forget-me-nots. By crossing a wobbly plank over the brook I would step onto a meadow of undulating hills. It smelled of wild grasses. I sat under a sprawling shrub and ate its red berries. Though not entirely sure they were edible, as nobody had taken a liking to them, I did not deign to ask an adult.

During the excursions to the meadow, following my grandparents' instructions not to be idle, I kept my eye on the hen and her chicks, so they would not run onto train tracks.

"We are not short on anything," I heard my grandma and grandpa say time and again.

Retro

Sounds were coming from the garderobe. Creaking, cracking, groaning. For some time she had been ignoring them. This morning she opened its doors wide and studiously eyed all her clothes which were arranged in utmost order. A dress in the color of fresh grass attracted her sight. It was a present from her first love.

She put on the dress and looked at herself in the mirror. The dress hugged her figure impeccably. She pranced through her room, admiring herself in the dated dress.

Suddenly a hole lit up in the fabric. She mended it neatly. The seam became almost invisible. Throughout the day she went in this dress everywhere, sometimes stepping into sentimental thoughts.

In the evening, news came.

Sounds no longer came from the garderobe.

Open Book

A crowd of people flowed down the street. They walked in a hurry, closely, one next to another to make it on time, to reach their destination, as cascades of new pedestrians joined in the stream. A woman walked against the current with a steady, dignified step. She did not look ahead, or to the sides, or at her shapely-heeled feet. A flowing skirt reached her slim calves, embracing her thighs. The afternoon rays stroked her face. Her eyes rested on the page of an open book that she was carrying. The crowd parted before her.

Closer

He spends days and nights in the lab trying to develop a pill for longevity. When dining and wining, more often than not his friends grill him about his findings. Everybody wants to sit close to the scientist.

"Have you made any progress since the summertime in the countryside?" asks a trim woman with a heaped plate of turnip greens in front of her.

"We are closer," the scientist says.

"Why would I want more of the same miserable thing?" says a man who swiftly forks a ruddy steak sprawled on his plate. "By the way, I've read somewhere that too much turnip greens can be quite treacherous."

"Really?" says the woman and suddenly chews her leaves less enthusiastically. "And how much closer?"

Bent over his viscid noodle soup the scientist swirls his spoon clockwise, then counterclockwise. He eats at a glacial pace. "It's all about manipulating proteins," he says. "Now we are writing a protocol to use pigs for experiments instead of rats."

"Most thrilling," says the turnip-greens woman, bashfully pinching two fries off her neighbor's dish.

"Please have more. French fries eaten from someone else's plate carry no calories," says the steak man, sweating at the hairline. "Fat is not such a threat, it's our lardy desires, permutations of ignorance and arrogance...."

"I wish I could create a pill for improving human nature," says the scientist. "In the meantime, let's have some spirit-forward drinks."

In Transit

The summer heat stabs the skin with needles. The usually assertive acacia tree, sky-gazing with its leafy symmetries, looks resigned. A man's hand glistens with sweat-beads as he scrolls up and down on his tablet. A little boy dressed in tennis clothes practices rotating-the-ball movements with his racket.

"When will the bus come?" the boy says.

"It will," the father says.

The boy rises on his toes, swipes the racket over his head and with a swift swing cuts through the thick air. "Do you like my serve?"

"Very much so, son." The man takes away his hand and eyes from the tablet, wipes the sweat trickling down his temples, and feverishly returns to his device.

The boy makes interchangeable spinning and clipping movements with his racket and starts singing: *"This land is my land, this land is your land…. So I'm gonna let it shine, let it shine, let it shine."*

"Daddy, do you like my music?"

"Yes, very much so." The man's voice sounds bouncy. The boy's mouth rounds up to a smile as he observes his father's busy profile. He runs up to the nearby iron gate and inspects the architecture of the spider web collapsed by the humidity and hums: *"This land is my land, this land is your land…. So I'm gonna let it shine, let it shine, let it shine."*

Gift

She received her voice from God. When she sang ballads, a drunkard sobered, a gossiper fell silent, feelings were born in a cynic.

She listened to advice from a man. She started taking voice lessons. Now she stands in a choir, beautifully carrying notes longer and higher, though nobody hears her.

She has lost her own voice. God silent.

Oceanness

The ocean flows eternally. Constant, yet not monotonous. Consistent, yet unpredictable. It fights, struggles, tears itself to smithereens. It crashes against rocks, spatters into droplets. It reclines gently on the sand. With its waters it sculpts mountains, with a thunder it smashes them into rubble. It disguises itself as an avalanche, burns in a white smoke, crawls like a lava to the shore. It roars, hisses, murmurs, quiets down to whisper, and recedes into the abyss. It never falls into habits.